WITHDRAWN

The Peanut-Free Café

by
Gloria
Koster

illustrated
by
Maryann
Cocca-Leffler

Albert Whitman & Company, Morton Grove, Illinois

Library of Congress Cataloging-in-Publication Data

Koster, Gloria.

The peanut-free café / by Gloria Koster ; illustrated by Maryann Cocca-Leffler.

p. cm.

Summary: When a new classmate has a peanut allergy and has to sit in a special area
of the lunchroom, Simon reconsiders his love for peanut butter.

ISBN 13: 978-0-8075-6386-1

ISBN 10: 0-8075-6386-2

[1. Peanuts–Fiction. 2. Food allergy–Fiction. 3. Schools–Fiction.] I. Cocca-Leffler, Maryann, 1958- ill. II. Title.

PZ7.K8528Pea 2006 [E]–dc22   2005024619

The design is by Maryann Cocca-Leffler and Carol Gildar.

For more information about Albert Whitman & Company, please visit our web site at www.albertwhitman.com.

Please visit Maryann at her web site: www.maryanncoccaleffler.com.

To my family—Eric, Megan, Charlie, and Alex—and
to my writing family—Claudia and Cathleen—G.K.

To Mrs. Karen Mcloud and all
her students—M.C-L.

Of all the foods in the world, Simon ate just four: bagels, green grapes, purple lollipops, and his favorite–peanut butter. Simon ate peanut butter every day for lunch. So did Zoe, Jared, Jaclyn, and Paul. Peanut butter was the most popular food at Nutley School. For Simon, peanut butter was essential.

So Good Peanut Butter

Dirt Bike Rodents

NOTE TO PARENTS AND TEACHERS

About one in twenty children suffers from a food allergy. Food allergy occurs when the body's immune system, the part of the body that is designed to fight infections, mistakenly attacks harmless food proteins. This "attack" may lead to a number of illnesses, the most common of which is a sudden allergic reaction. Mild symptoms of an allergic reaction can include an itchy mouth, hives and swollen skin, and nausea and vomiting. The more severe symptoms may include throat-tightening, trouble breathing, and problems with blood circulation leading to loss of blood pressure and unconsciousness. A severe food-allergic reaction is called "anaphylaxis" and this can, unfortunately, be fatal.

Although any food can cause an allergy, most are caused by eggs, milk, peanuts, tree nuts (such as walnut, cashew), fish, shellfish, wheat, or soy. Children typically outgrow most food allergies by school age, but allergies to peanuts, tree nuts, and seafood usually persist. Peanut allergy, in particular, has gained attention because allergic reactions can be severe, avoidance of food containing peanuts is difficult, and studies have shown a doubling of the number of children affected just within the past decade. It is now estimated that nearly one in one hundred children has a peanut allergy. We do not completely understand the reason for this recent rise in peanut allergy.

Successful management of a food allergy requires two key elements: measures to prevent ingesting the food, and maintenance of

an emergency plan in case of a reaction. These goals sound simple, but require preparation and teamwork. For schoolchildren, there must be a partnership between the allergic child, parents, school personnel, and even classmates to ensure safety. Everyone must understand the seriousness of the allergy—that a small ingestion could cause a severe reaction—and the many ways to avoid unintended ingestion of the food. Success depends upon policies of no food-sharing, and ensuring that any food considered safe has been prepared or provided by someone who understands nuances of ingredient-label reading and cross-contamination, which are pitfalls in avoidance of food allergens.

School personnel should understand and periodically review physician-prescribed emergency plans. These plans discuss recognizing allergic symptoms and the use of self-injectable epinephrine, a medication that improves circulation and breathing.

Most importantly, everyone must understand that children with a food allergy can do everything that other children can do, except eat the food to which they are allergic. With education, understanding, preparation, and teamwork, children with food allergies can and should live safe and happy lives.

Scott H. Sicherer, M.D.
Associate Professor of Pediatrics
Jaffe Food Allergy Institute
Mount Sinai School of Medicine, New York City

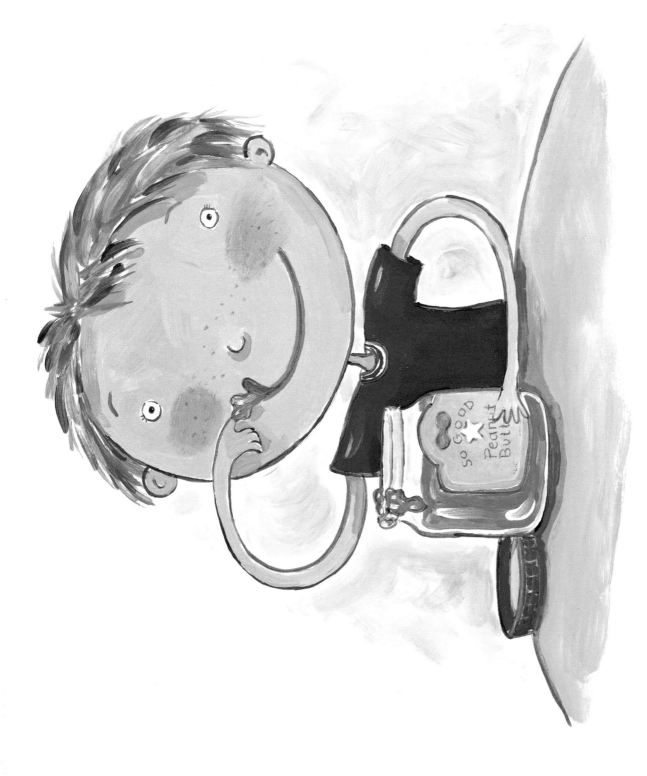

But after school and on weekends, Simon eats peanut butter. He likes to twirl his finger around the edge of the jar for a taste of the food that he still enjoys the most. For Simon, peanut butter is essential.

Of all the foods in the world, Simon now eats five. Every day his school lunch is reliably the same: half a bagel, a container of Texas Tilly's Ten-Bean Chili, a bunch of green grapes, and for dessert, a purple lollipop.

On Friday Simon finally joined Grant, Zoe, Jared, Paul, and Jaclyn. The friends sat together in the Peanut-Free Café. They laughed and talked. *Dirt Bike Rodents in the Amazon Rain Forest* was about to begin.

When she opened the
refrigerator, all she could find was a
pot of Texas Tilly's Ten-Bean Chili.
She scooped some chili into a plastic
container for Simon's lunch.

Thursday was a tough day. For the first time, Simon's peanut butter seemed tasteless.

At dinner Simon had no appetite. He went to bed early and tossed and turned.

The next morning he marched into the kitchen. "TODAY," he proclaimed, "I AM NOT GOING TO BRING PEANUT BUTTER TO SCHOOL! Please make me something different. Anything at all."

Simon's mother had been hoping for the day that Simon would try a brand-new food, but she had not gone to the supermarket all week.

On Wednesday Paul ate pizza. He was allowed to enter the Peanut-Free Café.

"Can't you at least try pizza?" Paul asked Simon.

"Please," called out Jared. "You're missing such a great movie!"

"Come on," Zoe added. "We saved you a place at our table."

But Simon sat by himself at the old table. He gazed longingly at the fun place that had been his very own clever idea.

Zoe's lunch was yogurt and berries. Jared had brought turkey and Swiss on a roll. "Welcome to the Peanut-Free Café," cooed Mrs. Hazel.

Jaclyn got the okay, too. Cream cheese and jelly had replaced her daily PB and J.

Only Simon and Paul were turned away. "No big deal," Paul reasoned. "We can see the second part of the movie tomorrow. And tomorrow is Pizza Day!"

"I don't eat pizza," mumbled Simon.

"Then bring something else," suggested Paul.

"Maybe fruit salad or soup. How about meat loaf?"

Simon did not eat any of those things. Of all the foods in the world, Simon ate just four, and for lunch, he needed to eat peanut butter.

"Not so fast," warned Mrs. Hazel, the lunch lady. "Before you enter the café, I must inspect all your lunches."

On Tuesday the Peanut-Free Café was open for business with baskets of popcorn, paper tablecloths, and crayons for doodling. Just like a real restaurant, the Peanut-Free Café had customers. Many Nutley students were ready to try something new, but not Simon. Even though it was his idea, Simon was definitely not ready.

As he and his friends walked into the lunchroom, the café lights dimmed.

"Hey, what's going on?" Simon demanded.

"Movie time!" responded a parent volunteer. "Dirt Bike Rodents in the Desert of Doom is about to begin in the Peanut-Free Cinema."

"Desert of Doom!" Simon exclaimed. "That's my favorite!"

He strode across the room, his peanut-butter lunch in hand. Zoe, Jaclyn, Jared, and Paul followed.

Announcing the Grand Opening of the Nutley Peanut-Free Café

Entertainment

Arts & Crafts

Snacks

Admission: A Peanut-Free Lunch

"Now there's a brilliant thought," agreed Principal Filbert, and at three o'clock a new flyer went home in every student's backpack.

On Tuesday the Peanut-Free Café was open for business with baskets of popcorn, paper tablecloths, and crayons for doodling. Just like a real restaurant, the Peanut-Free Café had customers. Many Nutley students were ready to try something new, but not Simon. Even though it was his idea, Simon was definitely not ready.

As he and his friends walked into the lunchroom, the café lights dimmed.

"Hey, what's going on?" Simon demanded.

"Movie time!" responded a parent volunteer. "Dirt Bike Rodents in the Desert of Doom is about to begin in the Peanut-Free Cinema."

"Desert of Doom!" Simon exclaimed. "That's my favorite!" He strode across the room, his peanut-butter lunch in hand. Zoe, Jaclyn, Jared, and Paul followed.

Announcing the **Grand Opening** of the Nutley **Peanut-Free Café**

Entertainment

Arts & Crafts

Snacks

Admission: A Peanut-Free Lunch

"Now there's a brilliant thought," agreed Principal Filbert, and at three o'clock a new flyer went home in every student's backpack.

"This will never do," declared Principal Filbert. "Boys and girls, we must think of a way to convince some children to join Grant at the peanut-free table."

"I could skip peanut butter tomorrow," suggested Zoe.

"Me, too," Jared offered.

"Grant is a really cool kid," said Simon. "But most kids at Nutley School don't know him. If the peanut-free table was a fun place, they might come. Then they'd get to know Grant better."

But at lunch his new friend sat at the peanut-free table . . . alone.

Peanut-free table

Grant chewed his tuna-salad sandwich. He swallowed his apple juice.

Across the room, his classmates laughed and talked.

On Monday morning Mr. Almond made Simon and Grant buddies. Grant was a whiz with numbers, and the boys finished their math before everyone else. When they discovered they were both fans of the Dirt Bike Rodents, they decided to write a story together.

"We can finish it at lunch," Simon suggested.

That afternoon Ms. Filbert paced back and forth in her office.

"Should I forbid peanut butter at Nutley School?" she wondered.

"That would make our school a safe place for Grant." But then the principal imagined the children of Nutley School going hungry day after day.

At three o'clock a flyer went home in every student's backpack. It said that on Monday there would be a peanut-free lunch table at Nutley School. Any child with a peanut-free lunch could sit there.

Peanut butter not allowed? The cafeteria fell silent.

Up and down the long lunchroom tables, the children of Nutley School gasped.

Simon was shocked. He had no idea that his favorite food could make someone so sick. He felt sorry for Grant and even sorrier for himself. What if peanut butter were no longer permitted at Nutley School?

"Because if I eat just one peanut or anything made with peanut oil, I can't breathe. I have to take my medicine right away." Grant placed his hand on his neck and pretended that he was choking.

Simon looked on in horror.

"At my last school," Grant continued, "nobody ever ate peanut butter. Peanut butter was not allowed."

"Sit down," Simon urged, but Grant just shook his head.

The new boy's mother gently drew her son from the lunchroom table as though it were a dangerous place. "Such polite children," she declared, "but I see you all enjoy peanut butter. I'm afraid that Grant can't sit with you."

"It's because of my peanut allergy," Grant explained. He reached into his backpack and pulled out something that looked like a fat pen.

"Cool," said Simon. "What's that?"

"It's my medicine," explained Grant. "It looks like a pen, but really it's a shot."

"A shot? Simon was afraid of shots. "Why do you have to have your own shot?"

"No, thank you," Grant replied.

"Have you eaten already?" inquired Principal Filbert.

"No," Grant whispered.

Simon adored lunch. Every day his lunch was reliably the same—peanut butter on a bagel, a bunch of green grapes, and for dessert, a purple lollipop. Parting with even a teeny bit of his meal was hard, but Simon remembered his manners. He tore off a piece of his sandwich. "Want some?" he offered.

One Friday, precisely at noon, a new student arrived at the main office. His name was Grant.

"Let's go meet some new friends," suggested Principal Filbert. She whisked Grant and his mother down the corridor and into the lunchroom, where the children had just begun to eat their peanut-butter lunches.

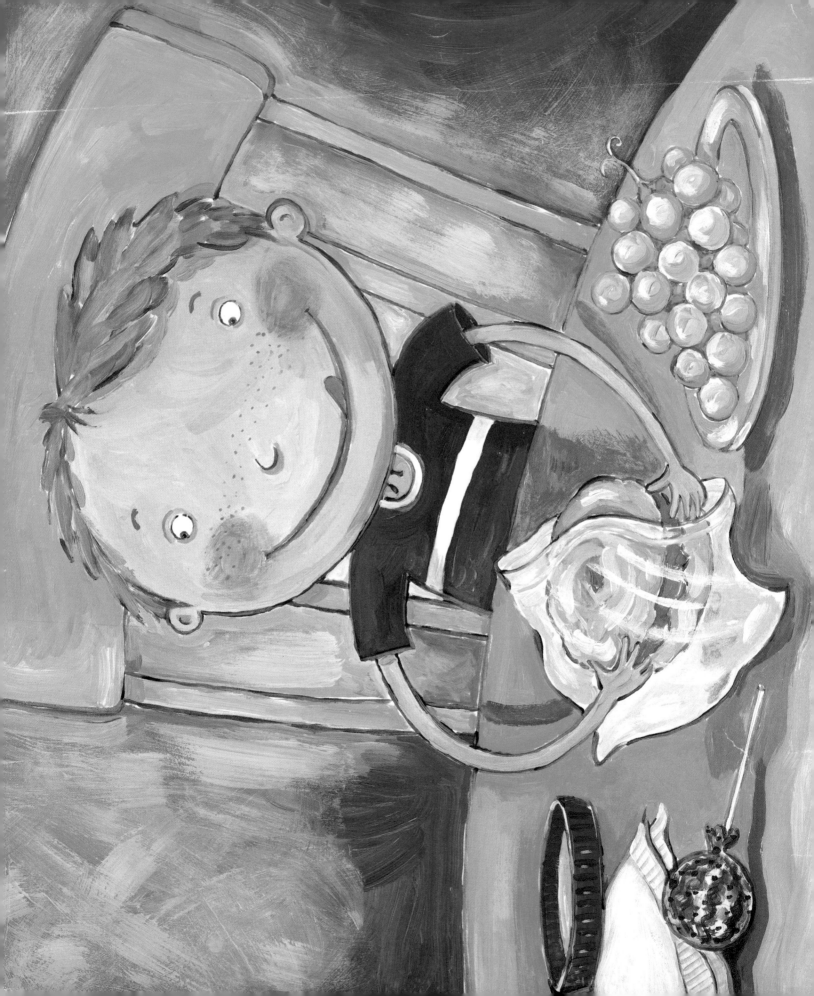